Who Swallowed Harold?
and other Poems about Pets

By Susan Pearson

Illustrated by David Slonim

Marshall Cavendish

New York London Singapore

Marshall Cavendish, 99 White Plains Road, Tarrytown, NY 10591
www.marshallcavendish.us

Library of Congress Cataloging-in-Publication Data
Pearson, Susan.
Who Swallowed Harold? and other poems about pets / by Susan Pearson;
illustrated by David Slonim.— 1st ed.
p. cm.
ISBN 0-7614-5193-5
1. Pets—Juvenile poetry. 2. Animals—Juvenile poetry.
3. Children's poetry, American. Slonim, David. II. Title.

PS3566.E23435D6 2005
811.54—dc22
2004020356

The text of this book is set in Bernhard Modern.
The illustrations are rendered in acrylic, colored pencil,
and ballpoint pen on 140-lb. hot-press watercolor paper.
Book design by Adam Mietlowski

Printed in China
First edition
1 3 5 6 2 4

Contents

Wishes

I built a doghouse without a dog.
I filled a litter box without a cat.
I fixed a birdcage without a bird.
I made a maze without a rat.

I have a super fishbowl ready.
I built a truly awesome hutch.
I lined a cage without a gerbil. . . .

I want a pet so awfully much.

Popcorn

Popcorn has a lot of poses.
When he's frightened, he plays dead.
When he's glad, he touches noses
and he naps on Buster's head.
When he's mad, his legs go stiff—
he clacks his teeth to give us warning.
But best of all is when he jumps
straight up for joy—then he's popcorning.

Though he's small, his joy is big.
Popcorn is my guinea pig.

Note: When guinea pigs jump straight up in the air,
it's called popcorning.

High C

Mario Mynah the Third
has the best tenor voice ever heard.
He sings opera at seven
and jazz at eleven—
it's hard to believe he's a bird.

Iguana

I have a pet iguana who
does not do very much, it's true:
spies a fly,
blinks her eye,
flicks her tongue
       ZAP!
then takes a nap.

9

Choosing a Dog

Great Dane, Beagle, Boxer, Bulldog,
Schnauzer, Poodle, Pekingese,
Dachshund, Newfoundland, Dalmatian,
Corgi, Chow Chow, Pug, Maltese,

Pinscher, Saint Bernard, Basenji,
Afghan, Bloodhound, Sheepdog, Pumi,
Whippet, Briard, German Shepherd,
Greyhound, Spitz, Hungarian Puli.

Irish Setter, Collie, Pointer,
Weimaraner, Shiba Inu,
Doberman, Chihuahua, Basset,
Cocker Spaniel, Kerry Blue.

All these breeds make me feel queasy. . . .

Choosing a dog isn't easy!

Do Goldfish Pee?

Do goldfish pee?
Got me!
Is the tank full
of fish wee-wee?
Do fish pee a lot?
Does it smell? Is it hot?
Will somebody tell me?
Probably not.

If goldfish pee,
then I have a notion
big fish in the ocean
probably pee a lot more.
So the next time that we
take a trip to the sea,
I think I will stay on the shore.

Mary Beth

Mary Beth, our snake, is missing—
we can't find her anywhere.
We keep listening for her hissing,
but it's neither here nor there.

Mom has gone into her bedroom,
shut the door, and won't come out
until our snake is safely captured.
Suddenly we hear her SHOUT!

We know for certain by the sound
that Mary Beth has now been found.

Old Tenzing

In the window sits old Tenzing,
remembering—
gazing through the windowpane,
thinking back upon his reign
as king of cats, prince of lords,
champion of howling hordes,
oak-tree climber, high-branch walker,
handsome youth, starling stalker,
fearless fighter, wisdom seeker,
swiftest runner, secret keeper.

Darkness falls. He leaves the sill
to pad across the kitchen floor
and curl up now beside the stove
to dream all night of days of yore.

A Collie Named William

William sits hour after hour
sniffing daisies and roses. No power
could get him to move.
He's stuck in a groove.
We call him our old collie-flower.

Who Swallowed Harold?

My brother swallowed Harold.
He did it on a dare.
I looked into the fishbowl
and Harold wasn't there.

I can't believe he'd do it
but my little sister Sue
saw him in the act
and swears that it is true.

My brother says he's sorry
for playing such a trick.
I bet he's only sorry
'cause Harold made him sick.

Busy Lizzie

Busy, busy is our Lizzie.
She is always in a tizzy.
Little mouth is yipping yapping.
Little feet are tipping tapping.
Racing chasing everywhere—
through the hallway, down the stair.
Underneath her, rugs are slipping.
Overhead the lamps are tipping.
      Skidding, scrambling,
      faster faster,
she is heading for disaster.
Plants are tumbling, vases smashing,
plates are falling, glasses crashing.
Guessing now that she's in trouble,
Lizzie's moving on the double,
sliding on the kitchen floor,
past the table, out the door.

Picky Eater

We found a cat—we named her Bounder—
but all she'll eat is fresh-caught flounder.
There's such a fishy smell around her,
we're wishing we had never found her.

Ant Farm

The ants are marching one by one.
It doesn't look like any fun
at all. They never look around,
they just keep looking at the ground.
They don't look happy when I'm there.
They do not ever seem to care
about a thing that I can see;
they clearly do not care for me.
I have no clue what they're about.
I think I'll throw my ant farm out.

24

A Ferret's Morning

1. Play hockey with a Ping-Pong ball.
2. Climb into a bag.
3. Tunnel through a sleeve and then
4. Play a game of tag.
5. Hide some food around the house.
6. Slide beneath a door.
7. Puff yourself into a ball.
8. Bounce across the floor.
9. Chase the dog.
10. Chase the cat.
11. Chase the vacuum after that.
12. And when you're tired and need a nap,
    find a bed on someone's lap.

Itchy Boris

Please don't sneeze—
you'll wake his fleas.

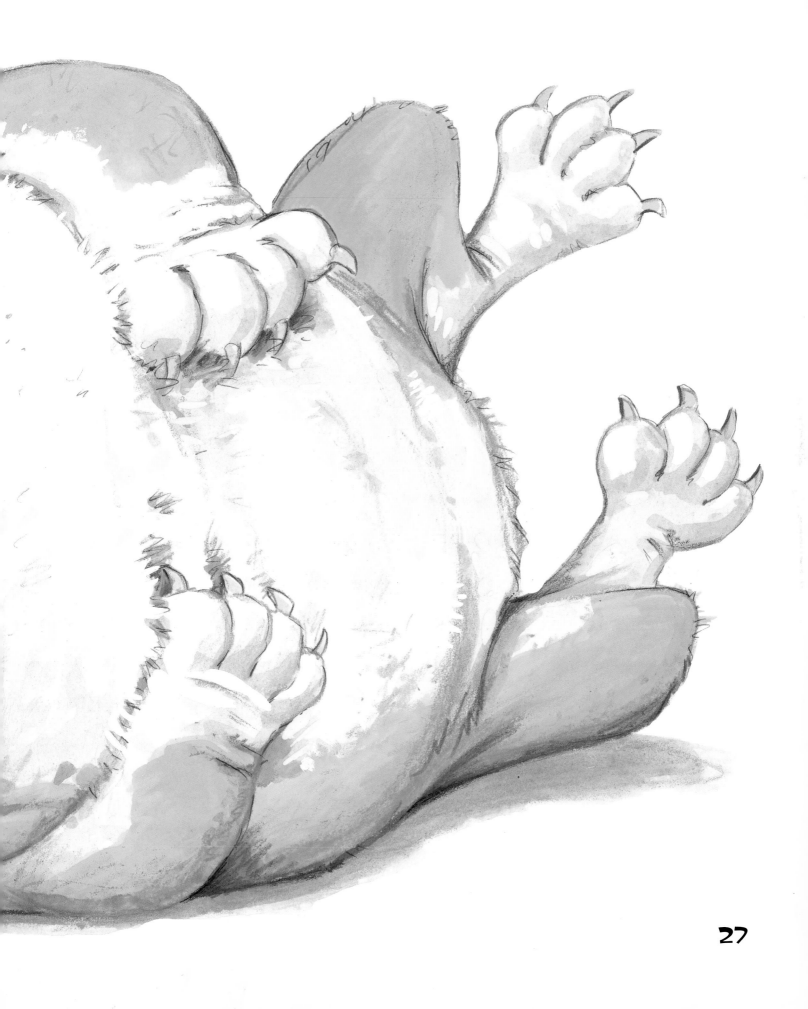

Gerald

Gerald, my pet rabbit,
is going through a phase.
He doesn't ever want to play.
He hasn't hopped in days.

He's looking very tired
and sticking to his hutch.
His pink nose barely twitches.
He isn't eating much.

But Gerald's getting fatter.
What could be the matter?

For days I haven't slept
a wink, I've been so tense.
But this morning when I checked,
it all made perfect sense!

Gerald has six babies—
one brown, two black, three white!
We now call Gerald Gerald*ine*,
and I can sleep tonight.

New Puppy

A puppy in spring
is a wonderful thing,
bursting with kisses and cuddles.
But open the door,
or else on your floor
you are likely to find several puddles.

My Turtle's in the Toilet

My turtle's in the toilet.
How he got there I can't think.
Did he climb up through the pipes
or jump down from the sink?

Did someone drop him in there
to play a joke on me?
How he landed in the toilet
is a mystery!

He's looking very cheerful
swimming round about
and not in any rush
for me to get him out.
PLEASE DON'T FLUSH!